Papa Jethro

BY Deborah Bodin Cohen

ILLUSTRATIONS BY Jane Dippold

KAR-BEN
PUBLISHING

For Arianna's G-pop Milton and PaPop Larry
who bring fun and love to grandparenting — D.B.C.

For my father, Bob,
and grandfathers, August and Leo — J.D.

Kar Ben Publishing, Inc.
A division of Lerner Publishing Group
241 First Avenue North
Minneapolis, MN 55401 U.S.A.

Website address: www.karben.com

Library of Congress Cataloging-in-Publication Data

Cohen, Deborah Bodin, 1968–
     Papa Jethro by Deborah Bodin Cohen ; illustrated by Jane Dippold.
        p.   cm.
     Summary: When Rachel asks her Grandpa Nick why he is Christian when she is
Jewish, he relates the biblical story of Jethro and his grandson Gershom, who loved
one another very much despite their different religious beliefs.
     ISBN-13: 978-1-58013-250-3 (lib. bdg. : alk. paper)
     ISBN-10: 1-58013-250-2 (lib. bdg. : alk. paper)
     [1. Grandfathers–Fiction. 2. Religions–Fiction. 3. Jethro (Biblical figure)
4. Gershom (Biblical figure)] I. Dippold, Jane, ill. II. Title.
PZ7.C6623Pap 2007
[E]–dc22   2006027431

Manufactured in the United States of America
1 2 3 4 5 6 – JR – 12 11 10 09 08 07

Author's Note

Each generation can find meaningful and timely lessons within the Torah's stories. Our generation is no exception. The Torah speaks to the diversity and complexity of today's Jewish families. Our great leader Moses married a non-Israelite woman named Zipporah. Some sages say that Zipporah converted to the Israelite religion, while others maintain that she remained true to her native Midianite faith. At the time of the Torah, however, religion was passed down through the father, and Moses and Zipporah raised their two sons, Gershom and Eliezer, within the Israelite tradition.

Jethro, Zipporah's father and a Midianite priest, helped care for the boys when Moses traveled to Egypt. After the Exodus, Jethro brought Zipporah and the boys to the Israelite camp. The Torah portrays Jethro as a wise, hospitable, and religious man. Jethro paid tribute to the God of the Israelites but returned to Midian before the Israelites received the Torah at Mount Sinai. Some sages say that Jethro converted to Judaism, while others believe that he was a righteous gentile. A seasoned leader, Jethro guided Moses on how to delegate responsibility and advised him on creating a judicial system.

Jewish tradition honors Jethro by giving his name *(Yitro)* to the weekly Torah portion that contains the Ten Commandments. Jethro appears several times in the Torah, including *Exodus* 2:16-22 and *Exodus* 18:1-27. Jethro has different names in the Bible, including Jether, Hobab and Reuel. As Hobab, he visited Moses and his family again in *Numbers* 10.

Rachel hugs Grandpa Nick as soon as he walks through the door.

"Be careful, my little girl! Don't hug me too tight. You don't want to crush the candy that I hid in my coat."

Grandpa laughs as he puts down his suitcase. "Are you ready to play? I have looked forward to hide-and-seek all day."

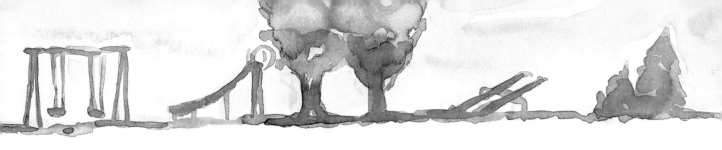

When Grandpa Nick visits Rachel, they paint with watercolors, play with model trains, and go to the park. Rachel and Grandpa Nick have just about everything in common, except she goes to synagogue and he goes to church.

Each night of his visit, Rachel likes to sit on Grandpa Nick's lap at bedtime and they talk. Rachel asks Grandpa Nick lots of questions. He often answers Rachel's questions with a story. Rachel loves her grandpa's stories.

One night, Rachel asks, "Why do I go to synagogue and you go to church?"

"Because we have different religions, my little girl. You are Jewish, and I am Christian," Grandpa Nick answers.

"But, you are my grandpa," says Rachel. "Shouldn't we be the same?"

"You ask good questions, my smart one. What story should I tell you to explain?" says Grandpa Nick, rubbing his chin while he thinks.

"I will tell you about a boy, just about your age, named Gershom. He had a grandfather he called Papa Jethro."

Rachel cuddles closer to Grandpa Nick.

"Gershom lived a long, long time ago in the hot, sandy desert near Egypt," Grandpa Nick begins. "You know who his daddy was. His name was Moses."

"Moses was a great Jewish leader," answers Rachel.
"He helped free the Jews from Egypt."

"Very good, Rachel. Moses was a wise leader and a great
prophet to all the people of Israel. But to Gershom, he was
simply 'daddy.' Gershom's grandpa was also a wise and
learned leader of a people called Midianites. But to Gershom,
he was simply 'Papa Jethro.'

"Papa Jethro and Gershom were of different religions, just like we are. Gershom was Jewish. Papa Jethro followed the Midianite religion."

"Why were they different?" Rachel asks, her eyes growing wide.

"Love is the answer to your question," says Grandpa Nick.

"When Moses was a young man, he became angry at how the Egyptians treated the Jewish slaves. He fled from Egypt and went to Midian. There he met Papa Jethro's beautiful daughter Zipporah. Moses and Zipporah fell in love, and even though they had different backgrounds, they married and started a family.

"Then God gave Moses a very important command: 'Go back to Egypt and lead your people to freedom.' Gershom, his mommy, and his baby brother, Eliezer, went with Moses to Egypt. But then the plagues began. Zipporah and the boys returned to Midian to stay with Papa Jethro.

"Gershom missed his father, but he was happy to have time to spend with Papa Jethro. Gershom and his grandpa liked to play games and tell stories, just like we do.

"When Papa Jethro heard that the Israelites had crossed the Red Sea to freedom, he brought Zipporah and the boys to meet Moses in the desert. Then Papa Jethro said good-bye to Gershom and his family and returned to Midian."

"Did Gershom ever see Papa Jethro again?" asks Rachel.

"Papa Jethro loved Gershom very much and missed him when they were apart," continues Grandpa Nick. "Sometimes Papa Jethro would visit Gershom and his family in the desert. As soon as he arrived, he would wink at Gershom and whisper in his ear, 'What game should we play first, my little boy?'

"Gershom and Papa Jethro played hide-and-seek just like we do. Papa Jethro found the best hiding spots, like standing tall and thin behind a camel's hump. Gershom and Papa Jethro also liked to play tag. Gershom could run faster than Papa Jethro, but sometimes Gershom would let his grandpa win."

Rachel giggles because sometimes she lets Grandpa Nick win at tag.

"Was it hard for Gershom to be Jewish while Papa Jethro was Midianite?" Rachel asks.

"Sometimes," Grandpa Nick says, hugging Rachel a little tighter. "But often they liked to share what made them different.

"When Papa Jethro came to visit, he always had delicious Midianite candies hidden in his bags. Gershom had to search to find them. Gershom knew many Midianite words, and Papa Jethro taught him a few more on each visit. Gershom and his grandpa pretended that Midianite was their secret code."

"I'd like to have a secret code with you, Grandpa," Rachel says. "It would be fun."

"Gershom told Papa Jethro all about being Jewish. He liked being the teacher. When he told his grandpa about lighting Shabbat candles and resting for a whole day each week, Papa Jethro closed his eyes and pretended to snore.

"Gershom tried to teach Papa Jethro how to blow the shofar. When Gershom blew it, the sound was loud and clear. When Papa Jethro tried, the only noise that came out was a 'peep, peep, peep.'

"Sometimes Gershom wished that his grandpa was Jewish. Once he asked, 'Papa Jethro, why don't you become Jewish, just like me?'

"'Being Midianite is very important to me,' Papa Jethro answered.

"Gershom thought for a moment and said, 'Then, I want to be Midianite, just like you.'

"'Being Jewish is part of you. I do not want you to change. I love you just the way you are,' Papa Jethro answered softly."

Rachel pulls back from Grandpa Nick and says, "Does it matter to you that I am Jewish and you are Christian?"

"Rachel, you are my granddaughter. Nothing else matters," answers Grandpa Nick. "I love you just like Papa Jethro loved Gershom."

Rachel hugs her grandpa. She wants to hear more about
Gershom and Papa Jethro, but she begins to yawn.

Grandpa Nick says, "If you teach me a few Hebrew words, we can have our own secret code. Do you know how to say good night in Hebrew?"

"It's *lailah tov*, Grandpa," Rachel answers. "I learned it in Sunday school."

"Then *lailah tov*, my little girl," Grandpa Nick whispers, kissing Rachel on her forehead and lifting her into her bed. *"Lailah tov."*

About the Author

DEBORAH BODIN COHEN is the Rabbi for Lifelong Education at Temple Emanuel in Cherry Hill, NJ. She is also the author of *The Seventh Day* and *Lilith's Ark*. She was ordained at the Hebrew Union College-Jewish Institute of Religion. She lives in Cherry Hill with her husband and young daughter.

About the Illustrator

JANE DIPPOLD graduated from Miami University of Ohio with a degree in Fine Arts. She has illustrated over 15 books for children with her lively, colorful artwork. Her art also appears in puzzles, games, and illustrations for children's magazines, as well as on greeting cards. Jane lives with her husband and three children in Coldwater, Ohio.